Mommy's Going to the Hospital

ISBN 0-9994628-6-5

Library of Congress Control Number 1-5318989361

Published by
HomeCooked Entertainment
Los Angeles, CA

Mommy went to the doctor, and was told she has a boo-boo deep inside her body.

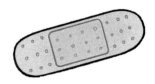

Now Mommy has to go to
the hospital, so that the
doctor can make her
boo-boo better.

At the hospital, the doctor and nurses will take good care of Mommy.

Mommy will be thinking of you, even when she's sleeping.

You might miss Mommy,
and it might make you sad
to not see her.

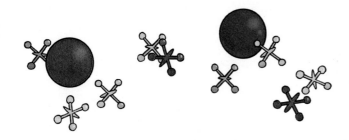

*It might make you angry
that Mommy isn't there to
play with you.*

But Mommy will be back soon, and when she comes home she'll show you her boo-boo.

Mommy will need lots of rest, and it might worry you to see her sleeping so much.

But every day
she'll get stronger.

And stronger...

And before you know it,
Mommy's boo-boo will be
all better!

55386570R00015

Made in the USA
San Bernardino,
CA